Pumpkin Spice Lane

THE SWEET SEASONS COLLECTION

KAYLA LOWE

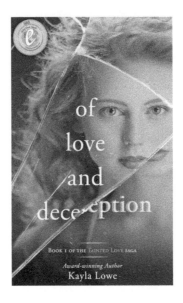

More of My Books

Sweet Honey by the Sea

The Beekeeper's Secret (Book 1)
A Royal Honeycomb (Book 2)
Bees in Blossom (Book 3)
Honeyed Kisses (Book 4)
Blooming Forever (Book 5)

Strawberry Beach Series

Beachside Lessons (Book 1)
Beachside Lessons (Book 2)
Beachside Lessons (Book 3)

Panama City Beach Series

Sun-Kissed Secrets (Book 1)
Sun-Kissed Secrets (Book 2)
Sun-Kissed Secrets (Book 3)

The Tainted Love Saga

Of Love and Deception (Book 1)
Of Love and Family (Book 2)
Of Love and Violence (Book 3)

Of Love and Abuse(Book 4)
Of Love and Crime (Book 5)
Of Love and Addiction (Book 6)
Of Love and Redemption (Book 7)

<u>Standalones</u>

Maiden's Blush

<u>Poetry</u>

Phantom Poetry
Lost and Found

Chapter One

The aroma of freshly baked pumpkin muffins wafted through The Cozy Cup as Eliza Frost twirled behind the counter, her curly red hair bouncing with each pirouette. She beamed at the familiar faces filling her café, her heart as warm as the steaming lattes she served.

"Who's ready for some Pumpkin Spice Lane Festival magic?" Eliza sang out, brandishing a whisk like a wand.

A chorus of cheers erupted from the regulars. Old Mr. Jenkins raised his mug in salute, while the knitting club in the corner clacked their needles in approval.

"I heard there's going to be a pumpkin carving

contest this year," piped up Jenny, a freckle-faced regular. "Are you entering, Eliza?"

Eliza winked, setting a plate of cinnamon rolls on the counter. "You bet your bottom dollar I am! I've got a design that'll knock your socks off faster than you can say 'jack-o'-lantern'!"

As laughter rippled through the café, Eliza's mind wandered to her plans for the festival. *Maybe I'll add some twinkling fairy lights to my booth this year*, she mused. *Or perhaps a talking scarecrow to greet customers? Oh, the possibilities!*

Her whimsical musings were interrupted by Mrs. Peabody, the town gossip, bustling through the door like a gust of autumn wind.

"Did you hear?" Mrs. Peabody exclaimed, her eyes wide behind rhinestone-studded glasses. "Barry Armstrong is back in town!"

The café fell silent. Eliza's stomach did a little flip, and not the good kind. She forced a smile, though it felt more like a grimace. "Barry Armstrong? Well, isn't that...something."

As the chatter in the café resumed, Eliza's mind drifted back to her high school days, when Barry Armstrong had been the star quarterback and the object of her secret affections. She remembered the way his sandy blonde hair caught the sunlight, the way his laughter echoed through the hallways, and how his smile could make her heart skip a beat.

They'd been close friends, spending long hours studying together in the library, sipping hot cocoa at The Cozy Cup, and volunteering side by side at the animal shelter. Barry had a way of making Eliza feel like she was the only person in the world, his green eyes twinkling with mischief and warmth whenever they shared an inside joke.

There had been moments, fleeting but precious, when Eliza thought that maybe, just maybe, Barry felt the same spark between them. The lingering hugs, the gentle brush of his hand against hers, the way he'd tuck a stray curl behind her ear—each gesture had set her heart aflutter with possibility.

But then came the day Barry announced he'd been accepted to a prestigious college in the big city. Eliza had plastered on a brave smile, congratulating him even as her heart splintered into a thousand pieces. She'd always known he was destined for greater things, but a selfish part of her had hoped that maybe, those greater things could include her.

The night before he left, they'd taken a walk through Maplewood's quaint streets, the autumn leaves crunching beneath their feet. Under the glow of the streetlamps, Barry had pulled Eliza into a hug, his embrace lingering a moment longer than usual. For a heartbeat, she'd allowed herself to imagine a future where he'd stay, where they'd explore the tantalizing "what if" that hung between them.

But the next morning, Barry was gone, taking a piece of Eliza's heart with him. She'd thrown herself into The Cozy Cup, channeling her emotions into baking the most delectable treats and creating a haven of warmth and comfort for her beloved community.

Now, years later, the mere mention of his name stirred up a whirlwind of memories and emotions. Eliza shook her head, trying to dispel the ghosts of her past. She was a different person now, confident and content in the life she'd built. Barry Armstrong might be back, but she refused to let his presence unravel the beautiful tapestry of her world.

With a deep breath, Eliza straightened her apron and turned her attention back to her customers, determined to focus on the present and the joy of the upcoming Pumpkin Spice Lane Festival. The past was the past, and she had a café full of smiling faces and pumpkin-flavored delights to attend to.

"They say he's some big-shot developer now," Mrs. Peabody continued, oblivious to Eliza's discomfort. "All suits and briefcases. A far cry from the boy who used to mow lawns for pocket money!"

Eliza's eyes instinctively rolled skyward. Of course, Barry Armstrong had to waltz back into Maplewood just when everything was perfect. She could almost hear the universe chuckling at her expense.

"Well," Eliza said, her voice a touch too bright, "I'm sure he'll find Maplewood exactly as charming as he left it. Now, who wants to try my new Autumn Spice Delight latte?"

As she busied herself with the espresso machine, Eliza couldn't help but wonder what Barry's return might mean for their sleepy little town. And why, after all these years, did the mere mention of his name still make her pulse quicken?

With a shake of her head, she pushed those thoughts aside. There was a festival to plan, after all, and no prodigal son was going to distract her from making it the best one yet.

Sarah leaned against the counter, her eyes twinkling with mischief. "So, Eliza...Barry Armstrong, huh? I seem to recall a certain someone doodling 'Mrs. Eliza Armstrong' in her math notebook."

Eliza nearly dropped the mug she was wiping. "Sarah!" she hissed, glancing around to make sure no one had overheard. "That was a million years ago. I was young and foolish, with terrible taste in boys and hairstyles."

"Mhmm," Sarah hummed, unconvinced. "And I'm sure your heart didn't skip a beat when you heard he was back in town."

Eliza huffed, tossing her dishrag onto her shoulder. "The only thing skipping is my patience. Barry Armstrong is ancient history."

But even as the words left her mouth, unbidden memories flooded her mind. Barry's crooked smile, the way he'd ruffle his hair when he was nervous, the butterflies she'd felt when he'd asked her to junior prom...

"Earth to Eliza!" Sarah waved a hand in front of her face. "You were totally daydreaming about him just now, weren't you?"

"I was not!" Eliza protested, feeling heat rise to her cheeks. "I was...thinking about pumpkin spice ratios for the festival."

Sarah opened her mouth to retort, but the jingling of the café door cut her off. Eliza looked up, her witty comeback dying on her lips as she locked eyes with none other than Barry Armstrong himself.

He stood in the doorway, backlit by the afternoon sun, looking unfairly handsome in a crisp button-down and dark jeans. His hair was shorter, his jawline sharper, but those warm brown eyes were exactly as she remembered.

"Eliza?" Barry's voice was deeper than she recalled, sending an involuntary shiver down her spine. "Eliza Frost, is that you?"

Eliza swallowed hard, painfully aware of Sarah's knowing smirk beside her. "Barry," she managed, her voice only slightly strangled. "Welcome back to Maplewood. Can I get you a coffee?"

Barry's lips curved into a slow smile as he approached the counter, his gaze never leaving Eliza's. "A coffee would be great, thanks. And maybe one of those famous pumpkin muffins I've been hearing about?"

Eliza busied herself with preparing his order, grateful for the distraction. Her hands shook slightly as she poured the coffee, and she silently cursed herself for being so affected by his presence.

"So, you're back in Maplewood," she said, aiming for casual but missing by a mile. "What brings you to our humble little town?"

Barry leaned against the counter, his posture relaxed but his eyes intense. "Business, mostly. I've got a new development project in the works. But I'd be lying if I said I wasn't looking forward to seeing some familiar faces." His gaze lingered on Eliza's, and she felt her cheeks warm.

Sarah, who had been watching the exchange with barely concealed glee, chose that moment to chime in. "Eliza was just telling me how excited she is for the Pumpkin Spice Lane Festival. You remember how much she loves it, right Barry?"

Eliza shot her friend a look that could curdle milk, but Barry just chuckled. "How could I forget? Eliza always had the best booth. And the best costume." He winked, and Eliza's traitorous heart skipped a beat.

"Well, I do love a good festival," she said breezily, handing him his coffee and muffin. "Speaking of which, I should probably get back to planning. Lots to do, you know."

Barry nodded, his expression unreadable. "Of course. I'll let you get to it." He hesitated, then added, "It's really good to see you, Eliza. I hope we can catch up more while I'm in town."

Eliza managed a smile, ignoring the butterflies in her stomach. "Sure, that would be...nice."

As Barry left, the bell above the door jingling in his wake, Sarah turned to Eliza with a gleeful grin. "Oh my god, the chemistry between you two! I could practically see the sparks flying!"

Eliza groaned, burying her face in her hands. "There were no sparks. Just...leftover static from high school, that's all."

But even as she said it, she knew it wasn't true. Barry Armstrong was back in Maplewood, and whether she liked it or not, things were about to get interesting.

Chapter Two

Eliza fidgeted in her seat at the town council meeting, her fingers drumming an anxious rhythm on the armrest. The old oak walls of the community center seemed to close in as Barry Armstrong stood at the podium, his polished presentation a stark contrast to the quaint surroundings.

"And with these modern updates," Barry's smooth voice carried through the room, "we can transform Maplewood into a bustling tourist destination."

Eliza's brow furrowed as she studied the sleek renderings on the screen. Gone were the charming storefronts and cobblestone streets, replaced by gleaming high-rises and trendy boutiques. Her heart sank as she realized the cozy town square—home to the beloved Pumpkin Spice Lane Festival—had been reimagined as a contemporary plaza.

Unable to contain herself any longer, Eliza shot to her feet. "But what about our traditions?" she blurted out, her cheeks flushing as all eyes turned to her. "The Pumpkin Spice Lane Festival isn't just an event. It's the heart of our community!"

Barry's confident smile faltered for a moment. "Eliza, progress doesn't mean losing what makes Maplewood special. We can incorporate-"

"Incorporate?" Eliza interrupted, her voice rising an octave. "You can't just 'incorporate' charm and history into a strip mall!"

A murmur of agreement rippled through the crowd. Emboldened, Eliza continued, "Our festival brings people together. It's about faith, family, and the simple joys of autumn. How can you put a price tag on that?"

As she finished, Eliza realized she was breathing heavily, her hands clenched at her sides. Barry's expression was unreadable as he cleared his throat. "Thank you for your...passionate input, Eliza. We'll certainly take it under advisement."

Back at The Cozy Cup, Eliza furiously wiped down the counter, muttering under her breath. "The nerve of that man! 'Take it under advisement.' As if our entire way of life is just a bullet point on his corporate checklist!"

Her longtime employee, Mabel, nodded sympathetically as she restocked the pastry case. "It's a crying shame, dear. This town's been just fine without any big city notions."

Eliza paused her cleaning, looking around at the warm, inviting café she'd poured her heart into. "You know what really gets me? He used to love this place as much as we do. What happened to that boy who helped me hang fairy lights for our first fall festival?"

Just then, the door chimed, and a group of regulars bustled in, their faces etched with concern. "Eliza!" Mrs. Henderson called out. "Tell us it's not true about tearing down the gazebo for one of them fancy coffee chains!"

Eliza's shoulders slumped. "I wish I could, Mrs. H. But Barry's got big plans for our little town."

As she filled them in on the details, a chorus of dismayed exclamations filled the air. Eliza felt a swell of affection for her neighbors, their shared worry oddly comforting.

"Well, I'll be," Old Joe huffed from his corner table. "Seems to me the Good Lord gave us all we need right here. Don't need no skyscrapers to be happy."

Eliza smiled, a determined glint in her eye. "You're absolutely right, Joe. And we're not going down without a fight. Who's with me?"

A resounding cheer filled The Cozy Cup, and for a moment, Eliza felt a flicker of hope. Change might be coming to Maplewood, but its spirit was as strong as ever.

The bell above the door jingled, and Eliza's heart skipped a beat as Barry stepped into The Cozy Cup. The café fell silent, all eyes darting between the two of them.

"Eliza," Barry said, his voice softer than she expected. "Can we talk?"

She plastered on a smile that didn't quite reach her eyes. "Sure, Barry. What can I get you? A venti corporate takeover with a shot of community destruction?"

Barry winced. "I deserve that. But please, just hear me out?"

Eliza sighed, wiping her hands on her apron. "Fine. Five minutes."

As they moved to a corner table, she couldn't help but notice how his cologne mingled with the scent of pumpkin spice in the air. It was infuriatingly pleasant.

"Look," Barry began, "I know my plans seem

drastic, but I truly believe they'll benefit Maplewood in the long run."

Eliza crossed her arms. "By replacing charm with chain stores?"

"By creating jobs, attracting tourists. We could put Maplewood on the map!"

"It's already on the map," Eliza retorted. "Right here." She tapped her heart.

Barry's eyes softened. "I remember that about you. Always leading with your heart."

For a moment, Eliza felt a flicker of the old connection between them. But she quickly squashed it.

"Well, someone has to," she said, standing up. "Your five minutes are up, Barry."

As he left, the tension between them was thick enough to spread on a scone. Eliza watched him go, her emotions a pumpkin spice latte of confusion—warm, spicy, and way too complicated.

Chapter Three

Eliza smoothed her skirt and took a deep breath as she entered the cozy community center, the scent of cinnamon and cloves wafting from a nearby diffuser. The festival committee members were already seated around the worn oak table, their excited chatter filling the room.

"Alright, folks," Eliza said with a bright smile, clapping her hands together. "Let's get this Pumpkin Spice Lane Festival planning underway!"

She unrolled a large sheet of paper across the table, revealing a meticulously drawn map of the town square. "I've sketched out some ideas for our traditional booths and activities. We'll have the pumpkin carving contest right here by the gazebo, and—"

"Ooh, I love the pumpkin carving!" Mildred, the town's retired librarian, exclaimed. "Remember when little Timmy Johnson carved that adorable lopsided cat last year?"

Eliza chuckled, her eyes crinkling at the corners. "How could I forget? That 'cat' looked more like a sentient blob with whiskers."

As the committee members leaned in to examine the map, Eliza's mind wandered. *Lord, please let this festival be a success. We need to show everyone that our traditions are worth preserving.*

"Now, for the pie-eating contest," Eliza continued, pointing to another spot on the map. "I was thinking we could—"

The door burst open, a gust of crisp autumn air sweeping into the room. Barry strode in, his cheeks flushed from the cool weather and his eyes twinkling with excitement.

"Sorry I'm late, everyone!" he announced, flashing that megawatt smile that always made Eliza's stomach do a little flip (much to her chagrin). "But I've got an idea that's going to knock your socks off!"

Eliza raised an eyebrow, trying to ignore the way her heart quickened. "Barry? What are you doing here? This is a closed committee meeting."

"Oh, come on, Eliza," he said, winking at her. "You know I can't resist a good festival planning session. Besides, I've got something that'll take this shindig to the next level."

He dramatically pulled out a colorful flyer from his jacket pocket and held it up for all to see. "Ladies and gentlemen, I present to you: The Pumpkin Spice Showdown!"

As the committee members oohed and ahhed, Eliza felt a twinge of anxiety. *Oh no*, she thought. *What is he up to now?*

"Picture this," Barry continued, gesturing grandly. "A competition where locals and visitors alike can showcase their best pumpkin spice creations. We're talking lattes, pies, candles—you name it! It'll bring in folks from all over the county!"

Eliza bit her lip, torn between admiration for Barry's enthusiasm and fear of change. "But Barry," she said cautiously, "our festival has always been about celebrating our town's traditions. We don't need to make it bigger or flashier."

Barry's eyes softened as he looked at her. "I know how much you love this town's history, Eliza. But sometimes a little change can be a good thing. Trust me on this one?"

As the committee members excitedly discussed Barry's idea, Eliza found herself caught between tradition and possibility. *Lord give me wisdom*, she prayed silently. And maybe the strength not to strangle Barry with his own scarf.

Eliza's eyes darted around the room, taking in the excited faces of the committee members. She couldn't deny the spark of enthusiasm Barry's idea had ignited, but her heart still clung to the festival's cherished traditions.

"Well," Mayor Thompson chuckled, his rotund belly jiggling, "I think we've got ourselves a real humdinger of an idea here!"

Mrs. Peabody nodded vigorously. "Oh yes, it could bring such life to our little celebration!"

Eliza took a deep breath, feeling the weight of expectation on her shoulders. "I suppose," she began hesitantly, "we could give it a trial run this year."

Barry's face lit up like a jack-o'-lantern. "That's the spirit, Eliza! We'll make it work together."

"Together?" Eliza's eyebrows shot up. "What do you mean?"

Mayor Thompson clapped his hands together. "It's settled then! Eliza and Barry, you'll co-chair this new Pumpkin Spice Showdown. Who better to balance tradition and innovation?"

As the meeting adjourned, Eliza's mind whirled. Co-chairs? With Barry? *Lord, give me patience*, she thought again as she snuck a glance at her new partner's grinning face.

Chapter Four

The next morning, Eliza found herself trudging through Mr. Wiggins' pumpkin patch, the earthy scent of autumn filling her nostrils. She plucked a small, perfectly round pumpkin from the vine, adding it to her overflowing wheelbarrow.

"These'll look mighty fine at the festival, Miss Eliza," Mr. Wiggins called from his tractor. The weathered farmer's kindly face crinkled with a smile.

Eliza managed a weak grin. "Thanks, Mr. Wiggins. I just hope the festival itself looks fine."

"Trouble brewin'?" he asked, climbing down from his perch.

She sighed, absentmindedly stroking a pumpkin's smooth surface. "Oh, it's just Barry. He's got all these big ideas for changing the festival. And now we're co-chairing this Pumpkin Spice Showdown thing."

Mr. Wiggins chuckled. "Change can be mighty scary, Miss Eliza. But sometimes the Good Lord uses it to grow us, like how these pumpkins need both sunshine and rain."

Eliza considered his words, gazing out over the patch. "I suppose you're right. I just worry we'll lose what makes our town special."

"Now, now," Mr. Wiggins said, patting her shoulder. "Seems to me, what makes this town special is the people in it. No fancy competition can change that."

As Eliza helped load pumpkins into her truck, she felt a small spark of hope. Maybe, just maybe, this Pumpkin Spice Showdown wouldn't be the disaster she feared. But working with Barry? That was a whole other kettle of fish.

Eliza drummed her fingers on the rustic wooden table, eyeing Barry across a sea of pumpkin-themed decorations. The Cozy Cup buzzed with its usual afternoon crowd, the aroma of cinnamon and nutmeg wafting through the air.

"So, I'm thinking we could have three categories for the Showdown," Barry said, his enthusiasm practically bubbling over. "Best Pumpkin Pie, Most Creative Pumpkin Carving, and—get this—Pumpkin Spice Recipe Innovation!"

Eliza raised an eyebrow. "Innovation? Isn't that a bit...much?"

Barry's grin widened. "That's the point! We want to draw people in with something new and exciting."

"But our festival has always been about tradition," Eliza countered, trying to keep her tone light. "People come for the comfort of familiarity, not...pumpkin spice innovations."

"Sometimes a little change can spice things up," Barry winked, clearly pleased with his pun.

Eliza groaned inwardly. Out loud, she said, "I suppose we could give it a try. But let's make sure we keep some of the classic elements too."

As they continued brainstorming, Eliza couldn't help but notice how Barry's eyes lit up with each new idea. It was...endearing, in a way. But still, she worried. Was all this change really necessary?

Their planning session was interrupted by Mabel,

the café's oldest regular, shuffling over with her walker. "I couldn't help but overhear," she said, her voice quavering with age but sparkling with mischief. "How about a pumpkin rolling race for us seniors?"

Eliza blinked in surprise. "Mabel, that's—"

"Brilliant!" Barry exclaimed, jotting it down. "We could have different age categories!"

Suddenly, the café erupted with suggestions from other patrons.

"Ooh, what about a pumpkin catapult contest?" called out Jimmy, the high school science teacher.

"Pumpkin spice latte chugging competition!" shouted Sally from behind the counter.

Eliza's head spun as she tried to keep up with the flood of ideas. To her amazement, she found herself getting caught up in the excitement. Maybe, just maybe, this could work after all.

Chapter Five

Eliza's heart raced as she stepped onto the makeshift stage in Maplewood's town square, the crisp autumn air nipping at her cheeks. She glanced at Barry, who stood next to her with his usual polished smile. *Lord give me strength,* she prayed silently. That was her constant prayer, it seemed—especially where Barry Armstrong was involved.

"Friends and neighbors," Eliza called out, her voice echoing across the sea of familiar faces. "We have an exciting announcement to make!"

Barry chimed in, his enthusiasm palpable. "Get ready for the first annual Pumpkin Spice Showdown!"

A ripple of excitement swept through the crowd.

Eliza couldn't help but smile, despite her reservations about working with Barry.

"We'll have pie-eating contests, pumpkin relays, and a pumpkin carving competition," Eliza continued, gesturing animatedly. "It'll be a celebration of all things fall and all things Maplewood!"

"And don't forget the grand prize," Barry added with a wink. "A year's supply of Maplewood's famous pumpkin spice blend!"

The townsfolk erupted in cheers and applause. Eliza's smile widened, her earlier doubts momentarily forgotten in the infectious joy of the moment.

As they stepped off the stage, Barry turned to her. "Well, that went well, don't you think?"

Eliza nodded, surprised to find herself agreeing with him. "It did. I think we might actually pull this off."

Later that afternoon, Eliza stood in her kitchen, surrounded by a cloud of cinnamon-scented smoke. She coughed, waving her oven mitt frantically to clear the air.

"Oh, for heaven's sake," she muttered, pulling out a blackened pie from the oven. "This is not how Grandma's recipe is supposed to turn out."

She set the ruined pie on the counter, her frustration mounting. Just then, a knock at the door startled her.

"Eliza? It's Barry. I thought I'd drop by to discuss some details about the showdown."

Eliza groaned inwardly. "Just a minute!" she called out, hastily trying to hide the evidence of her baking disaster.

As she opened the door, Barry's eyebrows shot up at the sight of her flour-covered apron and the lingering smell of burnt pie.

"Everything okay in there?" he asked, peering past her into the kitchen.

Eliza sighed, her shoulders slumping. "Let's just say my pumpkin pie skills need some divine intervention."

Barry chuckled, and Eliza found herself torn between annoyance at his amusement and a reluctant urge to laugh along.

Barry's eyes twinkled with amusement as he stepped into Eliza's kitchen. "Divine intervention, huh? Well, I'm no angel, but I might be able to help."

Eliza raised an eyebrow skeptically. "You? Mr. Corporate Suit knows how to bake?"

Barry rolled up his sleeves, revealing surprisingly toned forearms. "There's a lot you don't know about me, Eliza. Now, where's your flour?"

As Barry effortlessly moved around her kitchen, Eliza watched in astonishment. He expertly mixed ingredients, his hands working the dough with practiced ease.

"I can't believe this," Eliza muttered, more to herself than to Barry. "Where did you learn to bake like that?"

Barry grinned, sprinkling cinnamon into the pumpkin filling. "My grandmother. She always said a man should know his way around a kitchen as well as a boardroom."

Eliza's lips quirked into a reluctant smile. "Smart woman."

As they worked side by side, the kitchen filled with the warm, spicy scent of pumpkin pie done right. Eliza found herself relaxing, even laughing at Barry's corny baking puns.

"You know," she said, sliding the pie into the oven, "you're not half bad at this, Barry."

He winked at her. "Just wait until you see me at the Pumpkin Relay."

Chapter Six

The aroma of fresh coffee and cinnamon rolls wafted through Maplewood's community center as Eliza spread out a colorful array of flyers on the rickety folding table. She glanced up as Barry strode in, his boots clicking on the linoleum floor.

"Well, good morning, Sunshine," Barry drawled, tipping an imaginary hat. "Ready to plan the festival of the century?"

Eliza rolled her eyes, but couldn't suppress a smile. "I'll settle for a festival that doesn't end in disaster. Remember the Great Pumpkin Pie Incident of '09?"

Barry chuckled, leaning casually against the table. "How could I forget? Old Mrs. Henderson's dentures flying into the pie-eating contest. Classic Maplewood."

As they pored over the plans, Eliza found herself hyper-aware of Barry's presence. His arm brushed hers as he reached for a flyer, sending a jolt through her.

Stop it, she scolded herself. This is Barry. Annoying, infuriating Barry. Who just happens to smell really good today...

"Earth to Eliza," Barry waved a hand in front of her face. "You still with me?"

"Sorry," Eliza mumbled, flustered. "Just...thinking about logistics."

"Uh-huh," Barry smirked. "Well, while you were lost in la-la land, I had a brilliant idea for the dunk tank."

As Barry enthusiastically outlined his plan, complete with dramatic hand gestures, Eliza found herself captivated by his infectious energy. Had his eyes always been that shade of warm brown?

Later that afternoon, they stood in Eliza's rundown café, surveying the faded walls and chipped countertops.

"Well," Barry said, rolling up his sleeves, "let's get to work, partner."

Eliza's heart did a little flip at the word 'partner,'

but she pushed the feeling aside. "I hope you're as handy with a paintbrush as you are with festival planning."

As they worked side by side, painting and repairing, conversation flowed easily. Barry regaled her with tales of his college days, while Eliza shared stories of things that had happened in Maplewood since Barry had been gone.

"Remember old Mr. Wilkins and his prize-winning tomatoes?" Eliza laughed.

"How could I forget?" Barry grinned. "That man guarded those plants like Fort Knox."

As the afternoon wore on, Eliza found herself seeing Barry in a new light. His dedication to his tasks, his easy laughter, the way his eyes crinkled when he smiled...

No, she told herself firmly. *You're just caught up in the moment. This is still Barry, the guy who wants to change everything about Maplewood.*

But as they stood back to admire their handiwork, covered in paint and sharing proud smiles, Eliza couldn't quite convince her heart of that fact.

Just then, Rachel burst into the café, her eyes widening as she took in the freshly painted walls and the paint-splattered duo. "Wow, you two have been busy!" she exclaimed, a mischievous glint in her eye.

Eliza felt her cheeks warm. "Rachel! What are you doing here?"

"Can't a sister drop by?" Rachel's gaze darted between Eliza and Barry. "Though clearly, I'm interrupting something."

"You're not interrupting anything," Eliza said quickly, setting down her paintbrush. "We're just finishing up the renovation."

Barry cleared his throat. "I should probably head out. Thanks for the fun afternoon, Eliza." He smiled warmly at her before nodding to Rachel and departing.

As soon as the door closed behind him, Rachel pounced. "Oh my goodness, the sparks between you two! I could practically see hearts floating around your heads!"

Eliza rolled her eyes. "Don't be ridiculous. We're just working together on the festival."

"Uh-huh," Rachel said, unconvinced. "And that's why you're both covered in paint and grinning like lovesick teenagers?"

"I am not grinning like a lovesick teenager," Eliza protested, though she could feel the corners of her mouth twitching upward.

Rachel laughed. "Keep telling yourself that, sis. But I know you, and I haven't seen you look at anyone like that in years."

Eliza busied herself cleaning up paint supplies, trying to ignore the way her heart fluttered at Rachel's words. "You're imagining things," she insisted. "Barry and I are just...friendly colleagues."

"Right," Rachel drawled. "And I'm the Queen of England."

As Rachel continued to tease her, Eliza found herself both annoyed and secretly thrilled. Could Rachel be right? Was there something more than friendship brewing between her and Barry?

The next day, Eliza found herself walking alongside Barry, clipboard in hand, as they made their way through the fairgrounds. Colorful booths lined the path, each showcasing a different aspect of Maplewood's charm.

"So, what do you think?" Barry asked, gesturing to the festive scene around them.

Eliza couldn't help but smile. "It's coming together beautifully. I have to admit, your ideas really brought everything to life."

Barry's face lit up. "I'm glad you approve. Though I think your local knowledge was the real key to success."

Clearing her throat, she quickly stepped back. "We should, um, check out the craft booths next."

As they continued their tour, Eliza couldn't shake the warmth that spread through her chest every time Barry's arm brushed against hers or he leaned in close to share an observation. She found herself laughing more than she had in years, genuinely enjoying his company.

It wasn't until they reached the end of their circuit that Eliza realized they'd spent the entire afternoon together. It had felt so natural, so easy, that she hadn't even noticed the time passing.

"Well," Barry said, a hint of reluctance in his voice, "I guess that's everything."

Eliza nodded, surprised to find herself disappointed that their time together was coming to an end. "I suppose it is."

As they stood there, neither quite ready to part ways, Eliza couldn't help but wonder if maybe Rachel had been right after all.

And she wasn't sure how she felt about that.

Chapter Seven

As the crisp autumn breeze carried the aroma of cinnamon and nutmeg through the bustling fairgrounds, day one of the annual Pumpkin Spice Lane Festival kicked off with a bang. Colorful tents and booths lined the streets, showcasing an array of fall-themed treats and crafts. But the real buzz was about the highly anticipated Pumpkin Spice Showdown, the baking competition that had the whole town talking.

Eliza had finally ditched trying to recreate her grandma's recipe in favor of doing what she did best —her cinnamon rolls, famous for their gooey centers and perfectly balanced spice blend. They were sure to impress the judges.

As she set up her booth, arranging trays of

freshly baked goods and adjusting her apron, she couldn't help but feel a flutter of excitement in her chest.

Across the way, Barry was putting the finishing touches on his display. Eliza squinted. It looked like he'd made a pumpkin pie.

Very original, Barry, she thought.

The judges made their rounds, sampling the various pumpkin spice creations and jotting down notes. Eliza's cinnamon rolls received high praise for their perfect texture and bold flavors, while Barry's pie had the judges swooning over its velvety smoothness and just the right amount of sweetness.

As the judges deliberated, Eliza nervously fiddled with her apron strings. She glanced over at Barry, who seemed to be in deep conversation with one of the judges. A pang of jealousy shot through her. What could they possibly be discussing?

Finally, the head judge stepped up to the microphone. "Ladies and gentlemen, we have a winner!" The crowd fell silent, eagerly awaiting the announcement.

"In a stunning upset, the winner of this year's Pumpkin Spice Showdown is...Barry Armstrong, with his delectable pumpkin pie!"

The crowd erupted in applause, and Barry

stepped forward to accept his trophy, a grin spreading across his face. Eliza felt her heart sink. How could she have lost to Barry, of all people?

As the festivities wound down and the booths began to pack up, Eliza found herself face to face with Barry. "Congratulations," she said, trying to keep the bitterness out of her voice.

Barry smiled. "Thanks, Eliza. Your cinnamon rolls were amazing, by the way. I was sure you had it in the bag."

Eliza blinked in surprise. "Really? I thought your pie was the clear winner."

Barry shook his head. "Not a chance."

Despite her disappointment, Eliza found herself smiling. He was a gracious winner, and she felt chagrined for being a sore loser.

"See you at the Pumpkin Relay tomorrow?" he asked her.

She nodded. "You know it."

Chapter Eight

Eliza stood at the starting line of the Pumpkin Relay, eyeing Barry across the field. He'd traded his suit for jeans and a flannel shirt, looking disconcertingly at home in the small-town setting.

"Ready to eat my dust, Barry?" Eliza called out, adjusting her team's bright orange bandanas.

Barry grinned back, his team decked out in green. "In your dreams, Eliza!"

As the whistle blew, chaos erupted. Pumpkins flew through the air, some landing safely in waiting arms, others splattering on the ground.

Eliza raced forward, cradling a pumpkin like a football. "Come on, team!" she yelled, dodging a stray gourd. "We've got this!"

She couldn't help but laugh as she saw Barry, usually so composed, scrambling to catch a particularly enthusiastic throw from one of his teammates. The whole town seemed to be there, cheering and laughing as pumpkins soared and rolled across the field.

As she passed the baton—or rather, the pumpkin—to her next teammate, Eliza caught Barry's eye. To her surprise, he flashed her a genuine smile, his face flushed with exertion and joy.

For a moment, Eliza forgot about winning or losing. She was simply caught up in the laughter, the community spirit, and the sheer ridiculousness of grown adults playing relay with pumpkins.

As the relay reached its fever pitch, Barry's team was neck-and-neck with Eliza's. Barry sprinted across the field, arms outstretched to receive the pumpkin from his teammate. His eyes were locked on the orange blur hurtling towards him when suddenly—

SPLAT!

Barry's foot caught on a stray pumpkin stem, sending him careening face-first into a mountain of gourds. Pumpkin guts exploded everywhere as he disappeared into the pile with a muffled "Oomph!"

The crowd gasped, then burst into laughter.

Eliza, who had been running alongside Barry, skidded to a halt, her eyes wide with shock.

"Barry!" she called out, fighting back a giggle. "Are you okay?"

A moment later, Barry's head popped out of the pumpkin pile, his usually immaculate hair plastered with stringy orange pulp. He blinked, looking dazed for a second before a wide grin spread across his face.

"Well," he chuckled, plucking a seed from his ear, "I guess you could say I really fell for these pumpkins!"

Eliza couldn't help it—she doubled over in laughter. "Oh my goodness," she wheezed, offering him a hand. "That was quite the swan dive!"

As she helped Barry to his feet, Eliza noticed something change in her perception of him. The man standing before her, covered in pumpkin guts and laughing heartily, was a far cry from the stuffy businessman she'd initially pegged him as.

"You know," Barry said, wiping his face with a towel someone had tossed him, "I think I finally understand why this town loves its traditions so much. This is...fun."

Eliza raised an eyebrow. "Even covered in pumpkin innards?"

"Especially covered in pumpkin innards!" Barry laughed. "I haven't felt this carefree in years."

As they walked off the field together, Eliza found herself smiling. "You really do care about Maplewood, don't you?" she asked softly.

Barry nodded, his expression turning sincere. "I do. I know my ideas seem different, but I truly want what's best for this town. Contrary to what you might think Eliza, I didn't just leave Maplewood behind. I've always carried it with me."

Eliza felt a warmth spread through her chest. Maybe she'd misjudged Barry when he left all those years ago. And maybe, just maybe, Barry wasn't the enemy she'd thought he was.

The sun had dipped below the horizon, painting the sky in hues of orange and pink that reminded Eliza of the pumpkins scattered across the field. As they approached the edge of the town square, the festive lights strung between lampposts flickered to life, casting a warm glow over everything.

"I have to admit," Eliza said, breaking the comfortable silence that had settled between them, "you surprised me today, Barry."

Barry's eyebrows shot up. "Oh? How so?"

"Well, for starters, I didn't expect you to be such a good sport about your, um, pumpkin dive."

He chuckled, running a hand through his hair. "What can I say? The Lord works in mysterious ways. Sometimes He uses pumpkins to teach us humility."

Eliza snorted, then quickly covered her mouth, embarrassed. "Sorry, it's just...that's exactly the kind of thing my grandmother would say."

"She sounds like a wise woman," Barry said, his eyes twinkling.

They paused at the corner where their paths would diverge. Eliza found herself reluctant to end the evening, surprised by how much she'd enjoyed Barry's company.

"Listen," she began, fidgeting with the hem of her sweater, "I may have judged you too harshly at first. Your ideas for the town...they're not all bad."

Barry's face lit up. "Really? Does this mean you're coming around to the indoor pumpkin patch idea?"

Eliza laughed and shook her head. "Let's not get carried away. But I'm...open to hearing more."

"I'll take it," Barry said, grinning. He extended his hand. "Truce?"

Eliza hesitated for a moment, then took his hand. "Truce. For now."

As they shook hands, Eliza couldn't help but notice how warm Barry's palm felt against hers, and how his smile seemed to reach his eyes in a way she hadn't noticed before. She quickly pulled her hand away, suddenly flustered.

"Well, goodnight then," she said hurriedly. "See you tomorrow for the pie-eating contest?"

Barry nodded. "Wouldn't miss it for the world. Goodnight, Eliza."

As Eliza walked home, she found herself smiling, despite her best efforts not to. She wasn't ready to admit it out loud, but maybe, just maybe, Barry wasn't so bad after all.

Chapter Nine

The scent of freshly baked apple pie wafted through the air as Eliza and Barry took their places at the long table. Eliza's stomach growled, but she pushed away the hunger pangs. This wasn't about savoring the pie—it was about devouring it as quickly as possible.

"Ready to lose?" Barry teased, a twinkle in his eye.

Eliza shot him a playful glare. "In your dreams, city boy."

The whistle blew, and they dove in face-first. Eliza's world narrowed to nothing but sweet, gooey pie filling and flaky crust. She barely registered the cheers of the crowd as she shoveled handful after handful into her mouth.

Out of the corner of her eye, she caught a glimpse of Barry, his face covered in pie, working just as furiously. For a split second, their eyes met, and Eliza felt a flutter in her chest that had nothing to do with indigestion.

With a final, heroic effort, Eliza swallowed her last bite and threw her hands in the air. The crowd erupted in cheers as the judge declared her the winner.

Barry sat back, laughing and wiping his face. "I can't believe it. Beaten by a tiny little slip of a thing."

Eliza grinned, her own face sticky with pie. "What can I say? I'm full of surprises."

As they cleaned up, Barry gestured to a nearby table covered in pumpkins. "Ready for pumpking carving?"

Eliza shot him a grin. "You know it."

Eliza picked up her carving knife and set to work stabbing at her pumpkin—only to hear Barry tsking being her.

She looked up at him quizzically. "What?"

"Who taught you how to carve a pumpkin?" he teased, "Here, I'll guide you through it," he said as he leaned over her.

He positioned himself behind her, his hands

covering hers. Eliza's breath caught as she felt the warmth of his body against her back.

"First, we'll cut the top," Barry murmured, his breath tickling her ear as he guided her hands.

Eliza tried to focus on the pumpkin, but all she could think about was the closeness of Barry's body and the gentleness of his touch. A shiver ran down her spine, and she hoped he didn't notice.

"There, you just needed a little guidance," Barry said encouragingly as they finished the first cut.

Eliza laughed, trying to hide her flustered state. "I've managed to carve pumpkins all these years just fine, thanks."

"Well, now you know the right way to do it," he retorted.

Eliza rolled her eyes, but it was good-naturedly.

Barry went back to carving his own pumpkin. Eliza peeked at him, and as he made the final cut on the pumpkin's face, his knife suddenly slipped. "Ouch!" Barry exclaimed, jerking his hand back.

"Oh no!" Eliza gasped, spinning around to face him. "Are you okay?"

Barry held up his hand, a thin line of red appearing across his palm. "It's just a scratch," he said, trying to downplay it, but Eliza could see him wincing.

"Let me see," she insisted, gently taking his hand in hers. The touch sent a jolt through her, but she pushed the feeling aside, focusing on the task at hand. "We need to clean this. Come on."

Eliza led Barry to a nearby first aid station, her hand still holding his. "Sit," she commanded, pointing to a folding chair.

As she rummaged through the first aid kit, Barry chuckled. "You know, I'm usually the one giving orders."

Eliza raised an eyebrow. "Well, then you should know how to take them."

She found some antiseptic wipes and began cleaning the cut. Barry hissed at the sting.

"Sorry," Eliza murmured, her touch becoming gentler. "I guess I'm not as good at this as I am at eating pie."

Barry laughed, then winced again. "Hey, careful. Don't make me laugh while you're torturing me."

"Oh, stop being such a baby," Eliza teased, but her eyes were soft as she looked at him.

As she finished bandaging his hand, their eyes met. For a moment, neither of them moved.

"Thank you," Barry said softly.

Eliza felt her cheeks warm. "You're welcome," she replied, her voice equally quiet.

The sun was beginning to set as they walked back to the festival grounds. Eliza found herself stealing glances at Barry, noticing how the fading light caught his profile.

"You know," she said, breaking the comfortable silence, "I actually had a lot of fun today."

Barry grinned. "Even with my clumsy knife skills?"

"Especially with your clumsy knife skills," Eliza laughed. "It's nice to know you're not perfect at everything."

As they reached the edge of the fairgrounds, Eliza paused, looking out over the small town bathed in the warm glow of sunset. For the first time since Barry arrived, she felt a twinge of something...different.

Something she was afraid to put a name to.

"It's beautiful, isn't it?" Barry said softly, following her gaze.

Eliza nodded, surprised to find she meant it. "Yeah, it really is."

She glanced at Barry, who was still looking out at the town with a gentle smile.

She prayed he could see what she saw when she looked at it.

Barry turned to Eliza, his eyes soft and filled with

an emotion she couldn't quite place. The fading light cast a warm glow on his features, and Eliza found herself transfixed.

Slowly, almost hesitantly, Barry raised his hand to her face. His fingers were gentle as they brushed a stray lock of hair from her cheek, sending a shiver down her spine. Eliza's heart raced as he cupped her jaw, his thumb tracing the curve of her cheekbone.

"Eliza," he murmured, his voice low and filled with tenderness. "I..."

But before he could finish, Eliza found herself leaning in, drawn to him like a moth to a flame. Her eyes fluttered closed as she felt Barry's breath ghost over her lips. The world around them seemed to fade away, leaving nothing but the two of them in this perfect, quiet moment.

Just as their lips were about to meet, a sudden, shrill sound pierced the air. Eliza's eyes snapped open, and she jerked back, her heart pounding. It took her a moment to realize it was her phone ringing.

With fumbling hands, she pulled it from her pocket, seeing the name of one of the festival organizers on the screen. "Hello?" she answered, trying to keep her voice steady.

Barry watched her, concern etched on his face as Eliza's expression shifted from flustered to worried.

"What? No, no, I'll be right there," Eliza said hurriedly before hanging up. She turned to Barry, an apology in her eyes.

"There's an emergency at the festival. One of the booths caught fire and they need all hands on deck," she explained, already starting to move back towards the fairgrounds.

Barry caught her hand, stopping her. "I'll come with you," he said, his voice firm.

Eliza paused, looking down at their joined hands and then back up at Barry. Even in the midst of the chaos, she felt a warmth spread through her at his support.

She nodded, a small, grateful smile on her lips. "Okay. Let's go."

Hand in hand, they raced back towards the festival, the moment between them not forgotten, but put on hold as they faced the crisis together. As they ran, Eliza sent up a silent prayer, not just for the safety of the festival, but for the strength to face whatever this new feeling between her and Barry might bring.

The scent of smoke grew stronger as they approached the fairgrounds, the flickering of flames visible in the distance. Shouts and the wail of sirens filled the air, adding to the sense of urgency.

Eliza's grip on Barry's hand tightened as they pushed through the crowd, making their way to the center of the commotion. Her heart raced, but whether it was from the adrenaline of the moment or the lingering electricity of her almost-kiss with Barry, she couldn't be sure.

As they reached the booth in question, Eliza saw Pastor Tom and several other volunteers already working to douse the flames with fire extinguishers. The fire was small, contained to one corner of the booth, but the potential for it to spread was high.

"Pastor Tom!" Eliza called out, letting go of Barry's hand to rush forward. "What happened?"

The pastor turned, relief washing over his face at the sight of her. "Eliza, thank the Lord. It seems a faulty wire in one of the light strands sparked the fire. We're getting it under control, but we need to make sure it's completely out and that there's no risk of it reigniting."

Eliza nodded, already shrugging off her jacket. "Tell me what to do."

For the next several minutes, Eliza and Barry worked side by side with the other volunteers, making sure the fire was fully extinguished and clearing away the damaged materials. As they worked, Eliza couldn't help but marvel at how naturally she and Barry seemed to move together, anticipating each other's needs without a word.

It was Pastor Tom who finally called a halt, his hand coming to rest on Eliza's shoulder. "I think we've got it under control now," he said, his voice warm with gratitude. "You two have been a Godsend."

Eliza felt a flush of pride at the praise, but it was the look of admiration in Barry's eyes that made her heart skip a beat.

As the crowds began to disperse and the excitement died down, Eliza and Barry found themselves alone once again. There was a moment of awkward silence, the memory of their interrupted moment hanging in the air between them.

It was Barry who finally spoke, his hand coming up to rub the back of his neck in a gesture Eliza was beginning to recognize as a sign of nervousness. "Eliza, about earlier..."

But Eliza shook her head, a soft smile on her lips. "It's okay, Barry. We can talk about it later. Right now, I think we both could use a moment to catch our breath."

Barry looked at her, his eyes searching her face for

a long moment before he nodded. "You're right. But I do want to talk about it, Eliza. I...I think there's something here. Between us."

Eliza felt her heart swell at his words, a warmth spreading through her chest. "I think so too," she said softly.

They shared a smile, a promise of things to come, before turning to help with the clean-up. As they worked, Eliza found herself stealing glances at Barry, marveling at the turn her life had taken since he'd arrived in town.

She didn't know what the future held, but for the first time in a long time, she found herself excited to find out.

Chapter Ten

T he third night of the festival, a sudden darkness engulfed the festival grounds like a thick, inky blanket. Eliza's heart plummeted as the cheerful glow of thousands of carved pumpkins winked out, leaving only an eerie silence in its wake.

"Oh no, no, no," Eliza muttered, fumbling for her phone's flashlight. This can't be happening. Not tonight. Not during the Pumpkin Lighting Ceremony!

She stumbled through the crowd, her beam of light catching confused and disappointed faces. The warm scent of pumpkin spice that had permeated the air now seemed to mock her.

"Folks, please remain calm," Eliza called out, her

voice quavering. "We're experiencing a slight technical difficulty."

Slight? Who am I kidding? This is a disaster!

"Eliza!" Barry's voice cut through the murmurs of the crowd. She swung around, nearly blinding him with her phone light.

"Barry! The power's out. The ceremony—it's ruined!" Eliza's voice cracked.

Barry's face, half-shadowed in the dim light, set with determination. "Not if I can help it. Give me five minutes."

Before Eliza could respond, Barry vanished into the darkness. She stood there, frozen, the beam of her flashlight trembling.

Lord, please don't let this festival fall apart. We've worked so hard.

Suddenly, Barry's voice crackled over a megaphone. "Ladies and gentlemen, if I could have your attention please! We're working on getting power restored. In the meantime, let's make this memorable. Everyone, take out your phones and turn on your flashlights!"

A wave of light swept across the festival grounds as hundreds of phone flashlights flickered to life. Eliza's breath caught in her throat at the unexpected beauty of it.

"Now, let's have a Pumpkin Lighting Ceremony like no other!" Barry's enthusiastic voice boomed. "On the count of three, let's all shout 'Let there be light!' Ready? One, two, three!"

The crowd's voices rose in unison, "LET THERE BE LIGHT!"

As if on cue, a low hum filled the air, and suddenly, the festival grounds blazed with light. Cheers erupted as the pumpkins glowed once more, their carved faces grinning in the restored illumination.

Eliza spotted Barry next to a large generator, giving her a thumbs up. She rushed over, her eyes shining with gratitude and something more.

"Barry, I can't believe you did this! How did you—"

He grinned, running a hand through his tousled hair. "Let's just say I know a guy who knows a guy with a really big generator. Couldn't let your beautiful festival go dark, could I?"

Eliza's heart swelled with emotion. He'd thought of everything and been prepared with a back-up generator. "Thank you, Barry. You saved the night. That's something I've never thought about in all my years of festival planning."

Barry shrugged. "I'm used to thinking of all angles and being prepared," he said softly.

As they stood there, surrounded by the warm glow of pumpkins and the joyful chatter of the crowd, Eliza felt a spark of something new ignite within her.

Festival-goer after festival-goer came up to talk to them, amazed with the quick save.

Eliza couldn't help but beam at Barry, her heart fluttering as she watched him interact with the festival-goers. He seemed genuinely invested in the event, laughing with children and complimenting the intricate pumpkin carvings.

"You know," Eliza said, sidling up to him, "I think you might be the town hero tonight."

Barry chuckled, his eyes crinkling at the corners. "Oh, I don't know about that. I'm just happy to help preserve such a wonderful tradition."

Eliza's cheeks warmed at his sincerity. "Well, hero or not, I owe you one of my pumpkin spice lattes. It's the least I can do."

"I'd be honored," Barry replied, his smile causing Eliza's stomach to do a little flip.

As they strolled through the festival grounds, Eliza found herself stealing glances at Barry. She felt a pang.

Why did he have to leave all those years ago? They'd hadn't exactly been sweetheart all those years ago, but there'd been potential there.

And then he had to go and leave for the big city.

Lord, she thought, is this Your doing? Bringing him home?

Her musings were interrupted by the shrill ring of Barry's cell phone. He excused himself, stepping away to take the call. Eliza busied herself with adjusting a nearby display, trying not to eavesdrop, but Barry's excited tone caught her attention.

"Yes, that's right," she overheard him say. "The festival's been a huge success. I think we're in a great position to move forward with the development deal."

Eliza froze, her hand hovering over a miniature pumpkin. Her mind raced, piecing together Barry's involvement in the festival.

He'd only done this to try to push his deal. She should have known.

"We should be able to close soon," Barry continued, oblivious to Eliza's presence. "The town's support should be there now."

As Barry ended the call and turned back towards her, Eliza's heart sank. Had it all been a ploy? His charm, his helpfulness—was it just to gain the town's trust for his business deal?

Eliza's eyes stung with tears as she marched up to Barry, her fists clenched at her sides. "So that's what this has all been about?" she demanded, her voice quivering. "Using our festival to push through your development deal?"

Barry's eyes widened in surprise. "Eliza, I can explain—"

"Explain what?" she cut him off, her words sharp as autumn wind. "How you pretended to care about our town, about me, just to line your pockets?"

"It's not like that," Barry pleaded, reaching for her hand. Eliza jerked away as if his touch burned.

"I trusted you," she said, her voice barely above a whisper. "I thought you were different."

Barry's face fell. "Please, just let me—"

But Eliza was already turning away, her vision blurred by tears. She pushed through the crowd, ignoring the concerned looks from festival-goers. Her feet carried her to the safety of her café, where she collapsed into a chair, her heart feeling as hollow as an uncarved pumpkin.

The bell above the door chimed, and Eliza looked up to see her regulars filing in. Old Mrs.

Peabody's wrinkled face creased with concern as she settled into the chair beside Eliza.

"What's got you in such a tizzy, dear?" she asked, patting Eliza's hand.

Eliza's lip trembled as she recounted what she'd overheard. The café filled with a mix of gasps and murmurs.

Mr. Johnson shook his head.

"Should've known he didn't care about this town when he took off for the city all those years ago," grumbled Frank from behind his newspaper.

Eliza's mind whirled. "I just don't know what to think," she admitted, twisting a napkin in her hands. "He's done so much for the festival, for all of us. But what if it was all just...an act?"

Mrs. Peabody squeezed her hand. "Only the Good Lord knows what's truly in a person's heart, Eliza. Maybe there's more to the story?"

Eliza nodded absently, her gaze drifting to the window where fall leaves danced on the breeze. She wanted to believe in Barry, in the connection they'd shared. But how could she trust her own judgment now?

After everyone left and Eliza closed up shop, she sighed, her breath fogging up the café window as she stared out at the multicolored leaves swirling in the crisp autumn air. The whirlwind of emotions inside her matched the turbulent scene outside.

"Lord," she whispered, closing her eyes, "I could really use some guidance right about now."

She turned away from the window and found herself face-to-face with a framed photo of her grandmother, the café's founder. Eliza couldn't help but smile at the twinkle in her grandmother's eyes.

"What would you do, Gran?" she asked softly, tracing the edge of the frame.

Just then, Sandy, her bubbly teenage waitress, bounced over with a steaming mug. "I made you some of that pumpkin spice tea you love," she chirped. "Thought you could use a pick-me-up."

Eliza accepted the mug gratefully. "Thanks, Sandy. You're a peach."

As she sipped the comforting brew, Eliza's mind drifted back to Barry. His warm smile, his infectious enthusiasm, the way he'd swooped in to save the Pumpkin Lighting Ceremony...

"It just doesn't add up," she murmured to herself.

"What doesn't?" Sandy asked, cocking her head curiously.

Eliza hesitated, then decided to confide in the girl. "Barry. Everything he's done for the festival...it doesn't match up with someone who's only out for profit."

Sandy nodded sagely. "My mom always says there are three sides to every story—yours, theirs, and the truth."

Eliza blinked, surprised by the wisdom from her young employee. "Your mom's a smart lady."

As Sandy bustled off to serve other customers, Eliza found herself wrestling with a difficult question: Was she ready to hear Barry's side of the story?

Chapter Eleven

T he Pumpkin Spice Lane Festival's final night buzzed with energy, strings of twinkling pumpkin lights casting a warm glow over the town square. Eliza stood at the edge of the crowd, her heart pounding as Barry stepped onto the makeshift stage.

Barry cleared his throat, his normally confident demeanor replaced by nervous fidgeting. "Folks of Maplewood, I owe you all an apology," he began, his voice wavering slightly.

Eliza's eyebrows shot up. This was unexpected.

"I came here with intentions that weren't entirely pure," Barry continued. "But somewhere between the pumpkin pie contests and the hayrides, I fell in love—well, back in love to be exact." His eyes found

Eliza's in the crowd. "I grew up in this town, and I've rediscovered that love I had for it and...well, for someone very special."

A collective "aww" rippled through the audience. Eliza felt her cheeks flush, unsure whether to be flattered or mortified.

"That's why I've decided to pull out of the development deal," Barry announced. "Maplewood doesn't need changing. It's perfect just the way it is."

Gasps and murmurs erupted from the crowd. Eliza's jaw dropped. Was this really happening?

As Barry stepped down from the stage, people swarmed him with questions and congratulations. Eliza hung back, her mind whirling. Part of her wanted to rush over and hug him, but another part held her back.

"Well, that was quite the plot twist," her best friend whispered as she appeared at her side. "What are you going to do?"

Eliza shook her head, watching Barry field handshakes and back-pats. "I...I don't know," she admitted. "It's a lot to process."

"But isn't this what you wanted?" Maggie pressed.

"Yes...no...maybe?" Eliza sighed. "I mean, it's

incredibly sweet, but can I really trust that he's changed so quickly?"

As if sensing her gaze, Barry looked up and caught her eye. He offered a hesitant smile, a question in his eyes.

Eliza managed a small smile in return, but didn't move. She needed time to sort through the tornado of emotions swirling inside her.

"I think I need some air," she murmured to Maggie, slipping away from the crowd and heading towards the quieter outskirts of the festival.

The cool night air helped clear her head as she walked, the sounds of the celebration fading behind her. Barry's words echoed in her mind, warring with her doubts and fears. Could she really open her heart again, knowing how close she'd come to having it broken?

As she reached the old covered bridge at the edge of town, Eliza paused, leaning against the railing. The moon reflected off the river below, its gentle babbling a soothing counterpoint to her racing thoughts.

"Oh Lord," she whispered, closing her eyes. "I could really use some guidance right about now."

As if in answer to Eliza's whispered prayer, the soft strains of music drifted through the air. She turned, puzzled, as the notes grew clearer. It was her favorite hymn, "How Great Thou Art," but who could be singing it out here?

Eliza followed the melody back towards town, her heart quickening with each step. As she rounded the corner, she gasped. There, on the gazebo in the town square, stood the Maplewood Community Choir, their voices rising in perfect harmony.

"Then sings my soul..." they sang, their faces illuminated by the warm glow of pumpkin lanterns.

Tears pricked at Eliza's eyes as she watched townsfolk gathering, drawn by the unexpected performance.

She listened and watch the sight, her heart suddenly full to bursting.

How great thou art, indeed, she thought.

The bells on the café door jingled as Eliza stepped inside, her eyes immediately drawn to the lone figure seated at the table by the counter. Barry jumped up as she approached, nearly knocking over his chair in his haste.

"Eliza! I, uh, I wasn't sure when you'd come in," he stammered, revealing a slightly lopsided bouquet from behind his back. "These are for you. I know they're not exactly roses, but..."

Eliza couldn't help but smile as she took the bouquet of autumn-colored strawflowers. "Thank you, Barry."

As she sat down across from him, an awkward silence fell between them. Eliza fiddled with a napkin, trying to find the right words.

"Barry, I—"

"Eliza, listen—"

They both spoke at once, then broke off, chuckling nervously.

"You go first," Eliza offered, her heart pounding.

Barry took a deep breath. "Eliza, I know I messed up. Big time. And I'm so, so sorry. I came here thinking only about business, but you...you showed me what really matters."

Eliza nodded, her throat tight. "I want to believe you, Barry. I do. But how can I be sure?"

"Because I love you, Eliza Frost."

Barry reached across the table, taking her hands in his. "I love you, and I love this town. I was a fool to ever think I could change it—or that it needed changing at all. Maplewood is special because of people like you, who pour their hearts into making it a real community."

Eliza's pulse raced at his touch, his earnest words tugging at her heartstrings. "I love you too, Barry."

"I'm sorry I left you all those years ago," he added softly, his thumb stroking the back of her hand.

Eliza felt tears prick her eyes.

"Eliza," he went on, "I can promise you that I'll always try to do right by you, and by this town. You both mean everything to me."

Eliza searched his face, seeing the sincerity shining in his eyes. In that moment, she *knew*. Knew that this was real, that their love was worth fighting for. Worth taking a chance on.

"Well then," she said, a slow smile spreading across her face. "I guess you're stuck with me, Barry Armstrong."

His answering grin was brighter than all the pumpkin lights in Maplewood. "I wouldn't have it any other way."

He leaned across the table, and she met him halfway, their lips meeting in a kiss that held the promise of forever. Around them, the café seemed to glow even warmer, like a cozy haven shutting out the autumn chill.

When they finally parted, Eliza rested her forehead against his, savoring the moment. "So, what now?" she murmured.

"Now," Barry said, "I think I need to ask you to marry me."

Eliza's heart leapt into her throat. "Marry you?" she whispered, scarcely daring to believe her ears.

Barry nodded, his eyes shining with love and certainty. "I know it might seem sudden, but when you know, you know. And Eliza, I've never been more sure of anything in my life."

He slid out of his chair and dropped to one knee, pulling a small velvet box from his pocket. "I don't have a ring yet, but I do have this." He opened the box to reveal a delicate silver charm in the shape of a pumpkin. "It belonged to my grandmother. She always said she knew Grandpa was the one because he made her feel like she was home. And that's how I feel with you, Eliza. Like I'm finally home."

Tears streamed down Eliza's face as she nodded, too overwhelmed to speak. Barry slipped the charm onto the bracelet she always wore, his fingers lingering on her wrist.

"Is that a yes?" he asked hopefully, his voice rough with emotion.

"Yes," Eliza managed, laughing and crying all at once. "Yes, yes, a thousand times yes!"

Barry surged to his feet, pulling her into his arms and spinning her around. They laughed together, dizzy with joy and love.

As Barry set her back on her feet, Eliza cupped his face in her hands. "I love you, Barry Armstrong," she said, her heart in her eyes. "And I can't wait to be your wife."

"I love you too, future Mrs. Armstrong," Barry murmured, lowering his head to capture her lips once more.

And there, amidst the cozy glow of the Pumpkin Spice Café, Eliza and Barry sealed their love with a kiss—a heartfelt promise of all the sweet autumns yet to come.

Epilogue

TWO YEARS LATER

The aroma of pumpkin spice wafted through the crisp autumn air as Eliza adjusted the fall-themed bunting adorning Maplewood's main street. She couldn't help but smile at the sight of Barry across the way, his frame comically dwarfed by an enormous inflatable pumpkin he was wrangling into place.

"Need a hand there, pumpkin king?" Eliza called out teasingly.

Barry's face, flushed from exertion, broke into a grin. "I've got this under control, my cinnamon stick," he shouted back, just as the inflatable began to teeter precariously.

Eliza laughed, shaking her head. "Sure you do.

Just like last year when you ended up tangled in fairy lights."

As she made her way over to assist, Eliza marveled at how much had changed in just a couple of years. The Pumpkin Spice Lane Festival had blossomed from a quaint local event into a regional attraction, drawing visitors from all over to experience Maplewood's unique blend of small-town charm and modern flair.

"You know," Eliza said as they worked together to secure the giant pumpkin, "I never thought I'd say this, but I'm actually excited about the VR pumpkin carving contest this year."

Barry raised an eyebrow. "Oh really? What happened to 'real pumpkins or bust'?"

Eliza shrugged sheepishly. "What can I say? You've corrupted me with your newfangled ways. Besides, it means less mess to clean up."

As they stepped back to admire their handiwork, Eliza felt a warmth in her chest that had nothing to do with the spiced latte she'd consumed earlier. She thought about how seamlessly their lives had intertwined, much like the festival itself—a perfect fusion of tradition and innovation.

"Hey," she said softly, nudging Barry with her

elbow, "remember when we used to bicker about every little detail?"

Barry chuckled, wrapping an arm around her shoulders. "How could I forget? You were so stubborn."

"Me?" Eliza gasped in mock offense. "You were the one who wanted to change everything!"

"And we compromised," Barry retorted with a wink.

As they bantered, Eliza's gaze drifted down the street. The old-fashioned storefronts now sported sleek digital displays alongside their vintage signage. The smell of fresh-baked goods from Mrs. Henderson's bakery mingled with the enticing aroma of the new artisanal coffee shop.

"You know what?" Eliza mused, leaning into Barry's embrace. "I think we've created something pretty special here."

Barry nodded, his eyes twinkling. "Just like us, wouldn't you say?"

Eliza groaned good-naturedly at the cheesy line, but she couldn't deny the truth in it. As they stood there, surrounded by the fruits of their labor and love, she felt truly blessed. Who knew that a dash of pumpkin spice could lead to such a perfect blend?

Excerpt from Ruth

L ight filtered through the lace curtains, casting intricate shadows across the faded wallpaper. Ruth sat in the old wooden chair by the window, her hands folded in her lap. She gazed out at the quiet street, the stillness broken only by the occasional rustling of leaves in the gentle breeze. In the silence, memories flooded her mind, carrying her back to the life she had shared with her beloved husband.

She recalled their first meeting, a chance encounter at a bustling coffee shop. His warm smile and kind eyes had drawn her in, sparking a connection that would grow into something beautiful and profound. They had built a life together, navigating the joys and challenges that came their way. Through laughter and tears, triumphs and setbacks, their love had been the constant that anchored them.

But now, in the aftermath of his passing, Ruth found herself adrift, struggling to find her footing in this new reality. The weight of grief pressed heavily upon her heart, a constant companion that shadowed her every step. She yearned for his comforting presence, his gentle touch, and the sound of his voice that had always soothed her troubled soul.

With a sigh, Ruth stood and made her way to the kitchen, her footsteps echoing in the empty house. She opened the cabinet, reaching for a mug, but paused as her fingers brushed against the chipped one he had always favored. A bittersweet smile tugged at her lips as she remembered the countless mornings they had shared, sipping coffee and planning their day.

As she prepared her tea, Ruth's thoughts turned to the pressing matters at hand. The move to this small town had been a necessary step, a chance for her and Naomi to find solace and support in the close-knit community. Yet, the financial challenges loomed large, casting a shadow over their already fragile existence.

Ruth had spent countless hours scouring job listings, her hope dwindling with each rejection. The skills she had honed in the city seemed of little use here, where opportunities were scarce and competition fierce. She worried for Naomi, who had already endured so much loss, and the burden of providing for them both weighed heavily on her shoulders.

"Lord, please guide me," she whispered, her eyes closing as she leaned against the counter. "Show me the way forward, and grant me the strength to face whatever lies ahead."

As the steam from her tea curled upward, Ruth felt a flicker of determination ignite within her. She had weathered storms before, and with faith and perseverance, she would find a way through this one as well. For Naomi's sake, and for the memory of the love she had shared with her husband, Ruth would not give up.

With renewed resolve, she returned to the window, her gaze fixed on the horizon. The path ahead was uncertain, but Ruth knew that she would face it with the same quiet strength and resilience that had carried her this far. In this new chapter of her life, she would find purpose and hope, guided by the unwavering love that still lived within her heart.

The gentle creak of the floorboards announced Naomi's presence, and Ruth turned to see her mother-in-law's weathered face etched with concern. Naomi's eyes, once bright with joy, now held a shadow of the grief that had become their constant companion. She approached Ruth slowly, her steps measured and heavy, as if the weight of their shared sorrow had settled into her very bones.

"Oh, my dear girl," Naomi murmured, her voice a soothing balm against the silence. She reached out, her work-worn hands clasping Ruth's own, and in that simple gesture, a flicker of warmth passed between them. "I know the road ahead seems daunting, but you mustn't lose heart."

Ruth's throat tightened, emotion threatening to overtake her. She looked down at their intertwined fingers, drawing strength from the connection. "I just...I don't know how to make it right, Naomi. I've tried so hard to find work, to provide for us, but it feels like every door is closed."

Naomi's gaze softened, a sad smile tugging at the corners of her mouth. "You've already done so much, Ruth. More than I could ever have asked." She gently cupped Ruth's cheek, tilting her face upward until their eyes met. "Your love, your loyalty...it's a balm to my weary soul. You are a blessing, and together, we will find our way."

Tears spilled down Ruth's cheeks, and she leaned into Naomi's touch, allowing herself a moment of vulnerability. The weight of their shared grief hung heavy in the air, a palpable presence that seemed to seep into the very walls of their modest home.

"I miss him," Ruth whispered, her voice barely audible. "I miss the life we had, the dreams we shared. And sometimes...sometimes I fear I'll never find that kind of love again."

Naomi drew Ruth into a tight embrace, her own tears mingling with her daughter-in-law's. "Oh, my sweet girl," she murmured, her words muffled against Ruth's hair. "The love you and my son shared...it was a rare and beautiful thing. But I know, with all my heart, that you will find happiness again. You have so much light within you, so much to give."

As they clung to each other, the warmth of Naomi's love enveloped Ruth, a soothing balm against the ache of loss. In that moment, Ruth knew that though their path was marked by sorrow, they would face it together, drawing strength from the unbreakable bond they shared.

And somewhere, deep within her heart, a flicker

of hope began to grow, a tiny spark amidst the darkness. For even in the midst of their grief, Ruth knew that the love they had lost would forever be a part of them, guiding them forward into a future where healing and new beginnings awaited.

Keep reading Ruth here: Ruth

About the Author

Award-winning author Kayla Lowe writes women's fiction that explores complex themes with sensitivity and depth. Kayla's books delve into the intricacies of relationships, self-discovery, and resilience. From cozy love stories interspersed with a bit of faith to heartwarming tales of friendship and suspenseful novels of empowerment and heartbreak, her books illustrate the struggles specific to women.

When she's not churning out her next novel, you can find her with her feet in the sand and a book in her hand or curled up on the couch with her dogs.

Visit her website at www.authorkaylalowe.com.

Also by Kayla Lowe

<u>Series</u>

<u>Women of the Bible Fiction</u>

<u>Ruth</u>

<u>Esther</u>

<u>Rachel</u>

<u>Hannah</u>

<u>Deborah</u>

<u>Charms of the Chaste Court</u>

A Courtship in Covent Garden

Whispers in Westminster

Romance in Regent's Park

Serenade on Strand Street

Treasure in Tower Bridge

Of Love and Deception (Book 1)

Of Love and Family (Book 2)

Of Love and Violence (Book 3)

Of Love and Abuse(Book 4)

Of Love and Crime (Book 5)

Of Love and Addiction (Book 6)

Of Love and Redemption (Book 7)

Standalones

Maiden's Blush

Poetry

Phantom Poetry

Lost and Found

Milton Keynes UK
Ingram Content Group UK Ltd.
UKHW040306181024
449757UK00005B/352

9 798227 856272